Gypsy Mercer

Receding Tide

Gypsy Mercer

Receding Tide/Gypsy Mercer ~ First Edition
ISBN: 978-1-7325327-3-1

Dedication

Receding Tide is dedicated to two women who pull me from the tide whilst the tears flow. Both have taught me how to swim upstream.

MARTHA SMITH is always the voice of reason. She loves me enough to tell me the truth even when it hurts. She has been a friend and mentor over 25 years! She also makes a mean cornbread and a scrumptious lemon pie!

ASHLEY JANE gave me confidence and shared her experience and knowledge that enabled me to write and publish my first, and subsequent, books. She has played many roles, including editor, illustrator, cover creator, technical advisor, and cheerleader! She is brilliant!

Thank you Ladies from the bottom of my heart. You are the best!

My love always.

Gypsy

<u>Other books by Gypsy Mercer</u>

Into the Fire: Musings of a Gypsy Soul

(2018)

Surviving the Storm: Musings of a Gypsy Soul

(2019)

Falling Rain: Musings of a Gypsy Soul

(2020)

The Lone Wolf

(2020)

Virgo Unbound

(2021)

<u>Foreword</u>

Gypsy Mercer is a poet that only knows how to speak with her soul. If you have ever read her poetry, you know how she spills pieces of herself into her lines. You know the emotion imparted into each word. Her words have touched the hearts of thousands across social media. Her books sit in precious spaces in homes across the world. She has a beautiful style of writing that feels intimate, a confession whispered between two friends, between lovers, between two people drifting apart.

In this book, Receding Tide, Gypsy dives even deeper. It is about the push and pull, the rise and fall of new relationships, the give and take that comes with jumping in headfirst. The poetry pieces in these pages are equal parts euphoric and gut-wrenching. She deftly explains the high of riding that wave, the soft kiss of something new before delving into the way it all sweeps out to sea, leaving you heartbroken and bereft.

While I am always amazed by the emotions she effortlessly evokes, this book feels even more personal. The reader gets first row seats as she navigates a budding relationship, the first talks and smiles, the sweet interactions, the swept-away feeling that comes with finding a little piece of happiness...a perfect seashell brought right to you on the shore. Then we see the tide pull out, taking with it the joy and hope it once brought in. We see the way it leaves behind a barren shoreline, a heart once full now empty. It takes a strong person to stand firm in the face of pain, to refuse to give in and be pulled out to sea.

Each poem and prose piece in these pages is a reminder to find that strength within. That the moon will rise, and the tide will sweep back in.

And with it, perhaps we will find love and hope once more.

Ashley Jane
Bestselling Author of *All Darkness and Dahlias*

Part 1

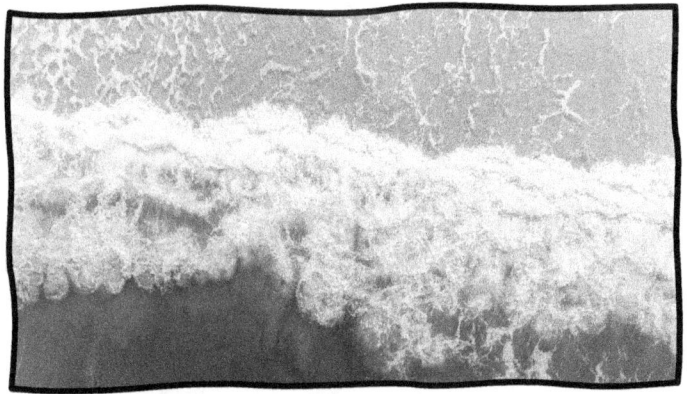

High Tide

Gypsy Mercer

You have no idea
How afraid I am
Of loving you
Because it means
Total surrender
And I am scared

———

Afraid

I need you

More

Than the air

    I breathe

More

Than the sun

    That warms me

More

Than the ocean

    That heals me

More

Than the moon

    That energizes me

More

Than the words

    Of a true poet

I need your love

    To live

Air

"Always"

Means forever

Say what you mean

Mean what you say

It is now or never

No in-between

———————

Always

I was your first love

You were mine

Young

Exciting

Passionate

But we were too young

To appreciate what we had

Life ensued

Separately

We found new loves

Tied in bows of deceit

Wrapped in promises

Taped together with hope

We both chose to lock the door

Never letting anyone that close

Again

Years happened

Our worlds were small

But safe

We thought we had healed

We tried again

Only to discover

Our brokenness

And inability to trust again

Heartbreak

Caved the wall of our dreams

Turning our love to dust

And our dreams to ash

―――――――

Ash

Gypsy Mercer

I crave something
I cannot name
It is just beyond my reach
I have bargained with the almighty
Promising feats and deeds
Beyond my grasp
    To know
    To understand
What I am missing within
My inner compass bids me caution
Yet I know no speed
Other than lightening
No corner I would not cut
No bridge I would not cross
No mountain I would not climb

For the answers
Buried deep inside me
   To know
   To understand
My heart

———————

Bargaining

I need to feel you

Discovering every line

Every peak and valley

Of your body

Of your mind

I want to know

Your smell

And your touch

As you explore me

In ways I have never felt before

I want to sense your moods

And your needs

Through your muscles

When taut

When relaxed

Feel the heat of your whisper

The electricity of your kiss

Feeling safe in your embrace
Know the pain of your absence
The love in your heart
Before I trust my feelings

Braille

Waiting for dawn to break

The monsters

The angels too

Lie in wait at night

To fill our dreams

Or taint our day

To help us find our way

Our fears and our hopes

Fight for supremacy

Deciding if our day

Is to be dark or bright

Nighttime magic

Gifting us answers

To questions

We were too afraid to ask

In the full light of day

As darkness fades to light

Breaking Dawn

I want to break free
>   Not sure what it looks like
>   Or feels like

Floating without boundaries

Actions without consequences

No expectations

No destinations

No waiting

No crying

Unbridled love

Unconstrained passion

No beginning

No end

Just a fantasy
>   Or dream
>   Or madness

Breaking Free

I burn with a passion within

For things never meant to be

I chase the dream

And sleep alone

Living my dream

———————

Burning

Restless

Waiting

For what

I know not

I sense something

  In the air

  In my thoughts

  In my chaos

I want to hurry it along

  Crack open the mystery

  Unwrap the gift

Let the universe be generous

I pray it is something

  I want

  I need

So peace once again returns

  When my mind is silenced

  And sleep embraces me

Chaos

Love is extraordinary

A rare jewel

In an otherwise ordinary life

The cherry on top of the sundae

The last touch

The last sigh

Before you release

Your mind to slumber

Cherish love

In its many faces and stages

It is worth remembering

Keeping on the shelf

For those private moments

When the lights go out

Cherish

I still call you up

With different scenarios

Of you coming back to me

I am wary but excited

We banter

No excuses

Nor explanations

Are offered by either of us

I listen intently

But even in my fantasy

I let you go

But why do you still return

The connection remains faint

Although not actionable

Guess the lesson was learned

———————

Return

Save the last dance for me

I will watch from the sidelines

As each ingénue

    Tempts you with her innocence

Each femme fatale

    With her veiled intrigue

Because I know

You will leave with me

The woman who knows

    Your every pleasure

    Teasing you with delights

You have only begun to imagine

    And long to experience

———

Dance

If Dante gave us circles of Hell
There must be an equal or greater
Number of circles of Heaven
It was in one of these circles
That I found you

———————

Dante

We can only love

To the depths of our understanding

Some days

    We are a bottomless spring

Other days

    An arid wasteland

We must come prepared

    Some days are sunny and bright

Filled with laughter and gentle touches

    Others are dark and cold

Where nothing grows

And we grow afraid

    Days change

    We change

Love has its own season

Changing with the wind

Sometimes caught

Sometimes not

_____

Depth

If you are but a dream

What a wonderful dream you are

I will protect you

Nourish you with love

Until life flows through you

And makes you tangible

Enough

To be my reality

And strong enough

To hold me

In your heart

———————

Dream

I am busy

Dreaming you

Into my life

————————

Dreaming

You lived in my imagination

A part of every dream

I have loved you fiercely

I have loved you madly

I keep looking for you

In every man I meet

Hoping I will feel a connection

I fear I have made you

More everything

I want you to be

And what I really need

Is a complicated man

To love a complicated me

———

Everything

I have been out of love

So long

I have forgotten

The gentle touch

The sweetness of a kiss

The salt of a tear

The feel of an embrace

My words now

More wrong than right

I am adrift

Love

Please find me

Sparking a flame anew

Resurrecting

My lost soul

Forgotten

You are a gambler

Playing with my heart

You ante in

With my expectations

Bet on my hopes

   And dreams

Pass the next round

Bet on my love

Call me on my fears

A full house

You as King of Hearts

Me as your Queen

———————

Gambler

Living in shadows

Some past

Some present

Disguised

Stealthily hiding from ghosts

Resurrected

Unresolved emotions

Needing to be untangled

In the brightness of the sun

Rejected or embraced

Breaking the chains

That hold you back

From loving anew

Or loving again

Your confusion lifted

Your soul at peace

Ghosts

I have claws
And Gypsy blood
That boils with passion
My eyes flash danger
At any lie
I move with grace and surety
Crawling under your skin
Assaulting your senses
Claiming your soul
Walk or run
To or from
Maybe you should play with a kitty
That doesn't leave marks

Gypsy Blood

I wish it had been you
Who taught me how to love
To love and be loved
It always
Should have been you

How to Love

Ahhh
It is you
I have been waiting
You always return
To remind me
Of the power
You wield over my thoughts
Both the good
And the sad

———————

It is You

We met when I was still naive

I appreciated all I saw

Years and a new introduction

Lit a fire within us

You were more than I expected

I was your willing pupil

Following our passion

In and out of bed

Knowing no bounds

Those are the days

I will always remember

Smiling in November

Magic

One day

You will catch me

I will have grown tired

    Of make-believe

    Senseless conversations

    Walking alone

    Unfinished sentences

    Tea for one

Your smile will unlock

    Missing pieces

    Unused parts

I will lean into you knowing

You will catch me

Before I fall

And I will pull you

Into the calm of my storm

Sharing our aloneness

Comfortably

Missing Pieces

Gypsy Mercer

Since you

I see moonlight and sunlight

In equal measure

Your smile brightens my day

During the evening

The twinkle in your eye

Captures the moonlight

My heart is yours to keep

Holding your hand

Sends ripples through my body

———————

Moonlight

The laughter

The wonder

I fell in love with you

In three days

Your dreams became mine

And you colored mine

With your understanding

I tasted the salt in your tears

You wiped away mine

Your laughter was addictive

Your eyes were hypnotic

When you spoke to me

In your special way

I believed in you

Just as I believe

I will find you once again

If only in my imagination

Once Again

I am dangerous
   Even
When I love you
I play for keeps

———————

Playing for Keeps

When going to war
Protect your fortress
Wear your armour
And your warrior face

When in love
Tear down the walls
Wear your heart
Leave your ego behind

———————

Prepare

Do not settle

If you are brave enough

To love

Fight for it

Be vulnerable

Be bold

Be honest

And when you do find it

And it is returned

Hold on for dear life

Love's fire will nurture you

And singe upon occasion

It is the magic you feel

It is the magic you give

Love's power is infinite

Not bound by time nor space

Carry it within

Others will see you shine

And it will give them promise

Promise

She was such a pretty poison
He was the devil's own
Their chaos was magic

———————

Pretty Poison

You broke my heart

To save your own

My love

With its intensity

And purity

Scared you

You did not trust

Your own

Knowing its vagaries

And inconsistencies

Would fail you

When needed most

To love me

Purity

She is quiet

She is surviving

    The test of time

Constantly reminding us

    That time flows forward

With our yearnings

    And our inspirations

We seek balance in our

    Highs and lows

'Tis the season for reflection

    And acceptance

Both come at a cost

    We are forced to pay

To participate in tomorrow

Reflection

Sometimes I retreat

And hold myself

Trying to save me

From your good intentions

Love me as I am

Not as you imagine me to be

We will both be happier

_____

Retreat

Rushing

Getting nowhere fast

Pedal on the gas

   To make the dash

Trying to catch a dream

Fading from memory

Making it a reality

Before the crash

Into the ghost garden

For eternity

———

Rushing

You hold a sacred place
Deep within me
Where unguarded emotions
Hide from light of day
You know my secrets
I know yours
It strengthens our bond
You call me out
When I lie to myself
I feed your ego
So you can see yourself
The way I do
We are as one
Untangling life's mysteries
Making our world
Safer

Safer

Gypsy Mercer

You lived in my heart

Before we even met

We laughed

We sparred

We shared our secrets

We had our own language

Meeting was anticlimactic

You were so familiar

I knew your every nuance

I heard every echo

Every whisper

I felt your thoughts

Like a warm breeze

You asked if I believed in soulmates

I said yes

And we continued

The romance that began

In our hearts

Secrets

Speak from your heart

I have no desire to be a casualty

Of misinterpreted words

If your words do not

Meet my desires

Let me be the one

To decide

If I go or stay

It is my choice to make

Yours to accept

Speak From Your Heart

Enter me spiritually

Make love to my mind

Make love to my heart

Make love to my soul

Make love to my body

Take me to a sacred world

    Made for two

Only then

Can you claim me

As your own

        Spiritually

I am not the calm in his storm

I am the storm

That opens his heart

_____

Storm

When I hold your hand

It is as if our puzzle has locked

Knowing that you know

That I know

That you feel the same

Forged in love

Totally complete

Because our stars

Have aligned

In a luminous supernova

For eternity

Supernova

Gypsy Mercer

There is a storm at my door

Boldly knocking

To be let in

Euphoria is peace

Rapture is passion

Why must I choose

When both satisfy my needs

In different way

On different days

Yet one pulls stronger

It requires the opposite

To exist

Choosing will be my undoing

The passion

The pain

Yet not knowing fire

Kills part of me

I must choose rapture

And never know peace

Storm Knocking

I promise

   ...not to tame you

      ...to love your wild

Tame

I want to flourish

Not just survive

Blue skies and sunshine

No clouds

No rain

I want to believe

And to forget

I need to know

Love is still possible

With this hole in my heart

Because I feel

My time has run out

And I am not through loving

I have more to give

And much more to receive

_____

Time

Why do you cry

Do your tears water

A garden within

Or drown your hopes and dreams

When the rain stops

Are you at peace

Or shattered beyond repair

Do tears fall

Because you feel nothing

Not even emptiness

Do you ever cry for something

You cannot name

You cannot touch

You cannot see

But know it is missing from you

Do you break your own heart

Wanting

Waiting

Praying

———————

Tears

You have taught me to dream

Again

I am beginning to believe

Again

I count days and hours

Again

And hold my breath for minutes

Again

I smile

A lot

I hug my dog

A lot

I forget what I am doing

A lot

I think of you incessantly

To Dream

Hours and minutes before I see you

My smile is wide and permanent

So many things fell in place

Just for us

I have run out of words

And am flying high on emotion

My imagination pictures your face

Your matching smile

I cannot wait

To taste our first kiss

Like a virgin

To this thing called love

I am all in

Let us see what more

Tomorrow can bring

That surpasses our today

Today

The waiting game

Is dangerous

In the silence

Fears

Hopes

Gain control

Walls resurface

Or erect anew

Patience falls by the wayside

Ready to pounce at disruption

Time loses dimension

Importance explodes

The outcome

Good or bad

Is the only salvation

———————

Waiting

Losing control

Wasting time

Going so slow

Wanna make you mine

Deep kisses

Hands roving

Promises made

Whispered in my ear

No holding back

Don't pull any stops

Take my body

Claim my heart

Never stop

———————

Wasting Time

My dreams always come back

To you

I want to fall back in love

With you

Recreate the magic

With you

My heart is on fire

For you

I am my best self

With you

I die a little each day

Without you

Tears fall

Without you

I cannot find peace

Without you

I want a life

With you

With only you

With You

Tomorrow never comes

To those who cannot see

The promise of tomorrow

So live your day to the fullest

Laugh and love with your whole heart

And enjoy what will be

Worry

I listen to your words

To know your truth

I see your actions

In them

I know your heart

I feel your love

———————

Your Love

I wonder

When your madness

Passes

Will there still

Be room for me

When twilight sets in

Will I still have a starring role

Or fade to pastel hues

To be forgotten

Until the next full moon

Your Madness

When I think of you

I am no longer alone

It is as though you touch me

Your smile breaths life

Into the depths of my heart and soul

Then I too smile

_____

Your Smile

Although your eyes
   Have a faraway look
Your mind is still on point
You are remembering
   Reliving past days
When life was easier
And your expectations high
When joy flowed more readily
Now your eyes focus
   And reality sets in
But your memories remain
And a smile appears
Reminding you
   When dreams were a reality
   Of a youth well spent
   And sacred beyond words

Youth

Gypsy Mercer

Part 2

Receding Tide

Gypsy Mercer

I do not know

What type storm you were

I only know

It turned my world upside down

Leaving me questioning

Everything

Except you

But your chaos was too much

Your storm

Left me stranded

On the beach

As the tide receded

Bruised and confused

And alone

———————

Receding Tide

His lies and demons

Are catching up

No longer hidden

Walking beside him

Tainting all thoughts

Poisoning all good

The aftereffects

Of a misspent life

Cheating love

After Effects

It has been a long time
Since I dreamt of you
It was peaceful
    Loving
It was nice
    Remembering
    Feeling love
Once again
When life was full
Of possibilities

_____

Again

She knows when to stop

Fighting herself

And give in

    To the tears

    To the fears

The memories live on

Time is not the cure

    Today

Is a victory

Knowing she walked away

From a lifetime of heartbreak

    Tomorrow

Is another story

After the fairytale ends

Another Story

You are not the type

Of man

For whom I will lay

Bare my heart

Your confidence

Leaves no room for error

You tolerate my missteps

As I do yours

But we both keep a tally

We give our best

Perfect enough

To get us through the night

While still remaining strangers

Until the next time

It is dark

And we are lonely

———————

Bare

My worst fears realized

Seeing you without blinders

    Ever so glad

    Ever so sad

Dreams into nightmares

Your smile disappeared

Along with your soothing voice

    Indignation

    Impatience

I met both

I thought so highly of you

Only to find a mere mortal

Hiding behind a mask

    Of respectability

Oozing charm

On a moonlit night

As the wolves howled

Blinders

Was it fear of losing

Or the need to win

Being too strong to quit

Or being too stubborn

That pulled me from the depths

Only to survive

The landmines

A wounded angel

Until the next lesson

Branded my heart

Scattered asunder

Until it finally made sense

Was it worth it

To discover

I made a mistake

Costing me my soul

My peace

My dreams

———————

Branded

Gypsy Mercer

She applied her makeup carefully

To mask any emotion

That tried to slip through

Her eyes were a problem

Moist from drowning in the depths

Of her shattered heart

His promises were a lie

His smile well practiced

His touch was gentle

And misleading

His kiss withheld

His love an illusion

She knew not why

When leaving

Her dreams were the last thing

To break

———————

Break

I breathe your love

I sense your taste

I miss your touch

Please...

Let me go

—————

Breathe

Your words were brutal

They cut like a knife

You are stuck in yesteryear

Still expecting perfection

From all you touch

Yet do not offer the same

You are lonely

But you lock your door

Come to me as you are

Tainted by life's lessons

Linger a little longer

Take time to unravel

We should give us

One more try

To finally know

If memories and dreams

And wishes are strong enough

To pull the best of us

From yesterday's ghosts

No more aborted tries

Face to face

Flesh to flesh

Separating fantasy

From reality

———————

Brutal Words

I keep thinking

That one day you will call

But you won't

All along

I thought I was the injured party

And you were stone

Little did I realize

You lost more

Than I did

I made you believe again

And that hurt worse

Than the pain of my broken heart

———————

Broken Dreams

You are paint-by-number

I use broad strokes

You analyze

I feel

You avoid cracks in sidewalks

I break my mother's back

We fill each other's gaps

With sighs

That rival a wolf's howl

We finish each other's sentences

If one retreats

The other follows

Our differences do not matter

Until they do

And the glue does not hold

———————

Cracks

Fearing the high euphoria brings

Knowing

The crash will surely follow

Feeling vulnerable

Before the attack

Yet unable to run

A penance I pay

For loving you

When I should have known

You were broken

And I am not

A Puzzle Master

And we were not a game

———

Crash

Open and inviting

Demanding your best

Offering my love

To heal

Wounds left by previous loves

Wanting you whole

To love me

But you did not believe

It was enough

That you were enough

To hold me

When dawn broke

———

Dawn

I thought I wanted more
But I could feel your lies
Beneath romantic dinners
While inhaling the Pacific
Cooking breakfast together
Walking trails at high noon
Picking favorite zebras
Sharing Italian entrees
Frozen tongues on ice cream
Sightseeing in the mountains
Digging rocks in the desert
Coffee at daybreak
It wasn't enough
To fill your emptiness
And my pain feeling it

Emptiness

She lay there

Remembering him

With a different ending

One where his lies

Were truth

And welcome

She imagined a life

Of loving and laughing

Secrets shared

Moments frozen in time

Kisses both gentle

   And passionate

Then she abruptly rose

Tears in her eyes

When she remembered

This was not how it was

Ending

I am the better person

Than you

Delivering compassion

With the denouement

I am kind yet firm

There is no dagger

In my arsenal

Unless you draw

First blood

I will act the lady

Laying no blame

At your feet

Why did you assume

My desire to talk

Meant a plea for your love

I have never begged for love

I wanted peace

Between us

Not the sword you thrust

Into my good intentions

Turning lovers to enemies

Piercing my heart

One last time

———————

Enemy

Gypsy Mercer

Will I ever say goodbye

To these memories

That live and breathe

Within me

Will I tire of the

Pain and sorrow

The exaltation

When I touch you

In my dreams

Only to wake empty handed

In the bed

We once shared

Must I forever

Be a slave

To this cache of love

Deep inside my heart

That knows no escape

———

Escape

How dare you
Withhold your love
How dare you
Refuse my love
Yet beg me to forgive
And try once more
Never
It is over
You are no longer
A person of interest
To my heart
Just a sad memory
I hope fades

Fade

Who were you seeing

When you looked at me

Your eyes were judgmental

Seeking out my flaws

I did not have a chance

To compete

With your idealized love

Nor could you live up to mine

It is better

We stopped

Before we really started

We were lonely

Living in a fantasy

That would not change

Nor could it last

Flaws

Don't lose focus

The thorns are real

And draw blood

———————

Focus

Your actions set me free

The answers were in your actions

I dreamt you into a demigod

Perfect divine love

The reality was different

Your embrace was stilted

Your kiss was cold and hard

You wielded words like swords

My psyche feeling the thrust

Leaving me too broken

To respond

My silence allowed
You to believe
Yet your insecurities
Were born in the darkness
Of your heart
Feeding your fears
Until only the calm hush
Of emptiness remained
Thus forfeiting me

———————

Forfeit

Gypsy Mercer

It was not meant to be

Was I that stubborn

That I missed the clues

Did I try to change me

To fit you

Did I sell my soul

For one last chance

Did my awakening

Have to be so cruel

A pain so deep

Tears refused to fall

Time eases pain

Clock hands move slowly

As I relive it all

In fractured images

With sharp edges

Fractured

No longer shackled and chained

    By your love

My flight no longer encumbered

    By your love

I rise before dawn

    Free once again

I breath pure air

    Free once again

I drink from the ocean

    Of life

To taste the nectar

    Of life

Resurrecting myself

    Free once again

Free

How can someone really say
    Goodbye
When they still live
    In your heart
They left a part of themselves
They can no longer control
It is yours now
Be gentle to yourself
And to your memories

———————

Goodbye

She will ride victorious

As dawn meets the day

She does not doubt

Her supremacy

In the battle

You began so long ago

She knows

You lost the battle

The day you forced her hand

And broke her heart

Because she could not love you

The way you deserved

To be loved

And you could not accept

What she offered

Her Offer

Gypsy Mercer

My heart locked on you

A long time ago

The warning flashers

We're invisible to me

Heart first

Head second

I was yours

I thought I was worldly

Until you opened my eyes

You loved being loved

I loved being loved by you

But it was not enough

The first time

Nor was it the last time

The sands of time emptied

On the bottom

Of the hour glass

Only dust and crushed dreams

Remain of us

Hour Glass

How quickly love turns
   To hate
When the illusions fade
A dream into a nightmare
A memory into a regret
Followed by anger
   For the stolen time
Forever lost
Hiding in your heart

Hiding

I do not dream any more

You demolished them

As you destroyed my imagination

You bled all color from rainbows

Stole the rumble from thunder

Leaving me shipwrecked

On an island of sand

Wet from my spent tears

Over your cruelty

And coldness

Imagination

One tear

Spoke more

Than a steady stream

A hurt so deep

My heart wept

As it deflated

Trying to save itself

From the assault

You visited upon it

With your indifference

———————

Indifference

If I could erase you

    From my memories

    From my thoughts

    From my heart

I could not

You were the essence

Of love as I knew it

Time will eventually fade

The details

But the hurt will remain

As a constant reminder

Of innocence lost

Innocence Lost

Receding Tide

Sometimes I retreat

Trying to save me

From your words

Uttered without thought

You do not know my triggers

Yet you seem to find them

And I yours

We thought starting fresh

Was best

But landmines keep erupting

Leaving us casualties

Of yesterday's wars

And the scars left behind

Landmines

Falling out of love hurt

Being in love

Was too painful

An emptiness

A caution remains

Will this be a lifetime lesson

Will healing ensue

Or leave me too scarred

Too scared

To let someone in

Does time really heal

Or is it all an illusion

Lessons

You broke your own heart

When you let me part

A million kisses

Holding hands

Yet you let me leave

Without saying a word

My perfume still in the air

My ring on the counter

My heart in your hand

The lock clicks loudly

As we come to the end

———

Lock

When trust is broken

So is the love

You once felt

It cannot be rebuilt

The structure has fallen

Debris so fragmented

Reassembly is impossible

Tears dry in their duct

The past is the past

Yet I feel your loss

Loss

I tell myself

I survived

The loss of a love

But he still exists

In fantasy

As I relive

The heartache

And the love

With a happier ending

That was not an ending

And pray

Memories fade in time

Loss of a Love

We had enough in common

To make a big mistake

We looked only surface deep

Where the laughter was plentiful

And passion ran deep

When we woke

We found ourselves laid bare

Our dreams

Our values

A mountain between us

The tears and regret

Our only connection

Not easily forgotten

Mistake

You are a monster

But not one of my making

Once open and loving

Now angry and vengeful

I hurt for me

I hurt for you

Someone as beautiful as you

Deserved a sacred love

Just as I

Deserved a sacred love

Not the deception

Nor the cruelty

You forced upon me

When I unknowingly

Gave you my love

———————

Monster

Gypsy Mercer

Lost in the mundane

No escape imminent

No vision of utopia

While lost in yesteryear

I followed the pebbles

Up steep mountains

Onto the sands

Welcoming the sea

Into the valleys

Scorching the earth

Until I found

And lost you

Life was never the same

Mundane

My Gypsy Soul spews fire and venom

At deceit

My Gypsy Heart breaks

Along with the bonds of trust

Although battle weary

I never drop the sword

That defends my honor and my life

My Gypsy Soul

Gypsy Mercer

Seduce my body
My mind is wary
Perhaps I will succumb
To the ecstasy
Your touch promises
While my mind battles
Other demons
From not so long ago
You demand my surrender
Half pleasure
Half pain
As I fight to hold on
To what was never meant to be

Never

Our time was over

Before it truly started

The window was small

I tried

You were not capable

Of opening your heart

It was still in pieces

Too brittle to remodel

I believed enough

For both of us

But it was not enough

To jump start

Your reluctant heart

———————

Not Enough

This time

I gave it all

The best of me

The vulnerable me

My love

My soul

It was not enough

For you

Finding you

Superficial

And unfeeling

No

We cannot be friends

Not Friends

The words we never said

Yet felt so deeply

Slipped away from us

Leaving us broken

Yearning for more time

But we had changed

Leaving our love in yesteryear

The death of our dream

The loss of an illusion

Once was not enough

But it was all

The world allowed us

———————————

Once was Not Enough

Gypsy Mercer

His words

Like a worn out record

Continue playing

In my head

Words I did not see coming

Set fire to my night

Burning all hope

Killing our past

Eliminating any future

As his body contorted in pain

I did not understand

Why his pain seemed more real

Than mine

But I felt his too

———————

Pain

Perfection was what you demanded
But not what you offered
You expect more than you give
You ask more than you answer
There is a beauty in flaws
You fail to see their uniqueness
Their special magic
How well they fit together
With imperfections
Two halves making a whole

———————

Perfection

Perhaps I waited too long

or you took my forever

———————

Perhaps

Clashing emotions

Hoping one wins

To calm this circus

This paroxysm of chaos

That disturbs my sleep

   My concentration

I need to move on

To the next fairytale

Where love wins

And the aching for you

   Ends

And the drowning

   Ceases

And the sun once again

   Rises

Leaving blue skies

Blue Skies

Gypsy Mercer

Lies fell off your tongue

Like sipping Courvoisier brandy

Both fiery and smooth

There was no hesitation

Since you believed every word

You were so smooth

From years of practice

Blind adoration

Was your expectation

You never dreamed

Two could play this game

You swallowed the cognac

Never tasting the poison

Of betrayal

On my sweet lips

Poison

It was God

Answering my prayer

With a resounding "No"

I did not want to listen

So he kept pounding

Until I understood

Not all dreams

Are meant to be

———————

Prayer

Gypsy Mercer

You had the power

Yet you failed

Your ego allowed no doubt

You heard only your own words

You lost my attention

When you could not hear me

And looked through me

As you sought a proper queen

Befitting your own sense of self

I wore no jewels

Nor raiment

Proclaiming my station

Trusting that a true king

Should recognize his soulmate

Among the multitudes

Vying for his love

But your heart was not pure

Leaving love forfeit

To your pretentious heart

———————

Pretentious

I promised you tomorrow
When I did not understand
Today
As it slowly slips away
I see the pain in your eyes
I want it to go away
I should have helped you
Understand my feelings
Not given you false hope
Heartbreak
And my guilt

———————

Promises

If I could cut you from my memory

Would my heart then be free

Or would I feel an emptiness

For something I cannot identify?

Would there be the same confusion

And melancholy

And urgency

To fill the void

Before I bleed out?

Or would I be carefree

Not knowing life's depth

And promise?

Question

Gypsy Mercer

She was a quiet witness

To his destruction

She watched him spiral

But knew not what to say

His actions

A plea

But she had no answers

She was not mute

Simply inexperienced

Not knowing how

To comfort him

She would not abandon him

All she could offer

Was her love

Her friendship

A constant reminder

That she cared

When all others forgot him

To lead separate lives

———

Quiet Witness

I am a Queen

Not your Queen

You are not strong enough

To be more than

A Court Jester

In my entourage

Of love

————————

Queen

Gypsy Mercer

I am at an impasse

I have condemned your actions

I have reviled your words

My shock silenced me

Saving you from lethal rebuttal

And me from shame

For participating in your games

Truth is not a weapon

In your arsenal

Though your aim

With your poisoned arrows

Pierced me deeper

And longer

Than I could have imagined

It was me

Who walked away

Head held high

With arrows still in my quiver

Quiver

The pain has gone away

Now it is habit

And wishful thinking

That bring you to mind

I woke up

Had an epiphany

Then everything

Fell into place

Understanding

Acceptance

Tied a ribbon around it

And tossed it out

Relegating it to history

Freeing my heart

Once again

Relegate

Love passed me by

I fed on its fire

Letting it consume me

Too many times

Allowing the Phoenix

To resurrect me

As my heartbeat faded

To ashes

I am not interested

In another love

And heartache

Instead

I sent him to you

For your revival

Or not

Revival

You stole the color from my life
After showing me

    Sunrises

    Sunsets

    The whitest shells

    Turquoise waters

    The reddest red roses

    The bluest eyes

You drained color from me
Now I only see shadows
Of what once was

    And for that

I will never forgive you

———

Roses

Did you think
   I did not care
When you told me
   It was over
There were no tears
   No recriminations
I looked at you
   And said okay
You did not realize
   I already knew
Because I was trying
   To tell you
The same thing
   Your ego
Never expected me
   To leave you

You did not realize
My parting gift
Was to let you believe
   It was your idea
Saving you the hurt
   Of losing my love

—————————

Saving You

Gypsy Mercer

I dreamt of you

In the warmth of the sun

All our wishes coming true

A love that was indestructible

By the outside world

We longed for our time together

Finally it was upon us

We were ecstatic

But you were not

Who I thought you to be

And I was not

Who you wanted me to be

And the ground froze

Fissures in our wake

Hard and fast

Freezing our dreams

In a schism of pain

Schism

The serenity of solitude

Seeks me

At unfathomable depths

Causing my surrender

On the most primordial level

But I am the Goddess

Of the Night

I take what I need

To survive

To fill my every need

Reigning supreme

———————

Serenity

Gypsy Mercer

Fade from my memory

Let me lock the door

Throw away the key

Let me be reborn whole

Without scars

Or missing pieces

As a reminder

Of love destroyed

By your disregard

For the gentle soul

Who nursed you back

From similar heartbreak

When someone equally unaware

Did the same to you

Leaving you shattered

And alone

Shattered

I am sad now

Remembering how invincible

I once was

And how boredom

Killed dreams

The adrenaline high

The ground crunching lows

Have eroded a shell

Making it smooth

As the tide undulates

And recedes into the sea

_____

Shell

Lashing out

With the steel whip of your tongue

Inflicting maximum damage

Your words were brutal

Gone was civility

It was a simple question

What did you react to

From your past

That you left me

Shell-shocked

Speechless

   and forever silenced

Shell-Shocked

The pain is gone

Yet the memories remain

I imagine happiness

Ignoring history

It is gentler that way

And I know it is a dream

From which

I have no desire to wake

And I accept that

The smile it left

On my lips

Is worth the illusion

———

Smile

Gypsy Mercer

The sky is falling said Chicken Little

An acorn became a tree

Neo takes the Red Pill

To be whom he must be

Alice looks down the looking glass

To see what she could see

The Riddler hides behind a mask

To free him from mediocrity

A poet masks her fears

Behind ambiguous words

To disguise her tears

To feel what she must feel

_____

The Looking Glass

This is me

The one who followed her heart

Up the stairs that led to sunshine

Breathing in peace and tranquility

Adorned by smiles

Clothed in love

I drank from the vessel

Satisfying my thirst

I envisioned eternity

But reality arrived in its place

Some things

    Are only meant for dreams

I slipped through the passage

    Tentatively

Took my first step into the corridor

The light was not as bright

But curiosity lit my way

With each footfall

A sureness followed

This was meant to be

Colors matched in hues

  Of blue and green

Peace overcame me once again

The smiles were laughter pouring

   From my eyes

This felt right for a time

Until I found another stairwell

This led down

Each step became darker

Yet I felt no fear

The air grew warmer

And sizzled with promise

And expectations

My soul unleashed

As I dove into brilliant
   Reds and purples
Answering my hearts needs

I now understood
I needed to feed me
To see me whole
To survive

———————

This is Me

Thoughts of you

Are fewer and farther between

The intensity is waning

Until it is not

When I am caught

Unaware

And I am back

To yesteryear

Again

———————

Thoughts of You

Time has run out
The hourglass has emptied
We were our best
    Together
For so long
Friends and lovers
It does not get better than that
    Conversations
    Confidences
Meeting behind our masks
We filled every minute
But our time ran out
Leaving us
With sublime memories
Etched upon our soul

Time Ran Out

Gypsy Mercer

I cannot decide

Does time move fast

Or slowly

Do you still think of me

Or have I been dispatched

To far off corners

Only visited when lonely

Or when reminded of me

It is only fair if it is so

Time was dragging

So to save myself

I did the same to you

I still remember

Every detail

Of our time together

But now the burning pain

Is controlled

Except when it is not

Time Together

If I could do it all over again

I would not

To be free

Of these memories

And dreams

Would be my only gain

Yet new dreams

Would search for you

———————————

To Be Free

It is too late

Time did not stop

With your departure

It was one time too many

Access to me is not a revolving door

I am sorry I let you believe that

I truly believed in us

This time

Your words cut like a knife

You severed our love

With one slice

Too Late

I am so damn tired

...of loving you

_____

Tired

Gypsy Mercer

I trusted you

And I never trust anyone

I remain braced for disappointment

Yet you slipped in

With your sincerity

And clumsiness

Making me believe

You were real

My walls dropped

My love grew

But I saw you crumble

Before me

No longer your princess

I became your enemy

And you mine

Ever polite

We smiled as strangers

Until we could pretend no more
We walked away
Arms full of broken dreams
And shattered promises

———————

Trust

Gypsy Mercer

I am trying

But my attention wanders

You are bright

You are funny

I enjoy our time together

But I am not engaged

I am wasting your hours

And your minutes

The wall, the pain, the memory

Have locked down my heart

He still lives in my head

As I attempt to remove

The last visages of him

Leaving no room

For another love

While he still breathes

Trying

If we are not meant to be

Fade from my memory

Let me lock the door

Throw away the key

Let me be reborn

In trust

Whole

And not fear your knock

Or your plea

Immune to your efforts

Cleansed and new

A virgin at love

Like the first time

I opened my heart

To you

———————————

Virgin

Gypsy Mercer

You asked me

When was the last time

I trusted someone

I paused, thinking

I did not remember

The mind continues to search

In the quiet

The answer was there

Clear

Painfully clear

One September morning

It just knew

I told him I trusted him

Completely

I was euphoric

Wait until we know each other

Better

So cryptic
I filed it away
And forgot

I should have walked away

_____

Walk Away

Alone now

Missing us

Love was not enough

To heal our broken parts

We learned this

The hard way

As we tried

Holding on

It was never simple

Between us

But I loved us

For trying

We Tried

Caught in his web

This assassin of my psyche

I could not dream

I could not escape

Death came slowly

In my gilded cage

The web was strung too tightly

For me to leave

But it unraveled

Freeing me

   To imagine

   To create

   To experience

A world once lost

Now regained

I was reborn a warrior

In a world of my making

Web

Gypsy Mercer

You have not seen the last of me

You will glimpse me in a blur

    Rounding the corner

Writing poetry

    And remember

Drinking wine

    And smile

Her kiss will not be the same

    And you will hesitate

Her touch is not a breath

    Nor a promise

    Against your skin

I appear to you

In a whisper

When you try to forget

Because I still hold your heart

    In mine

———————

Whisper

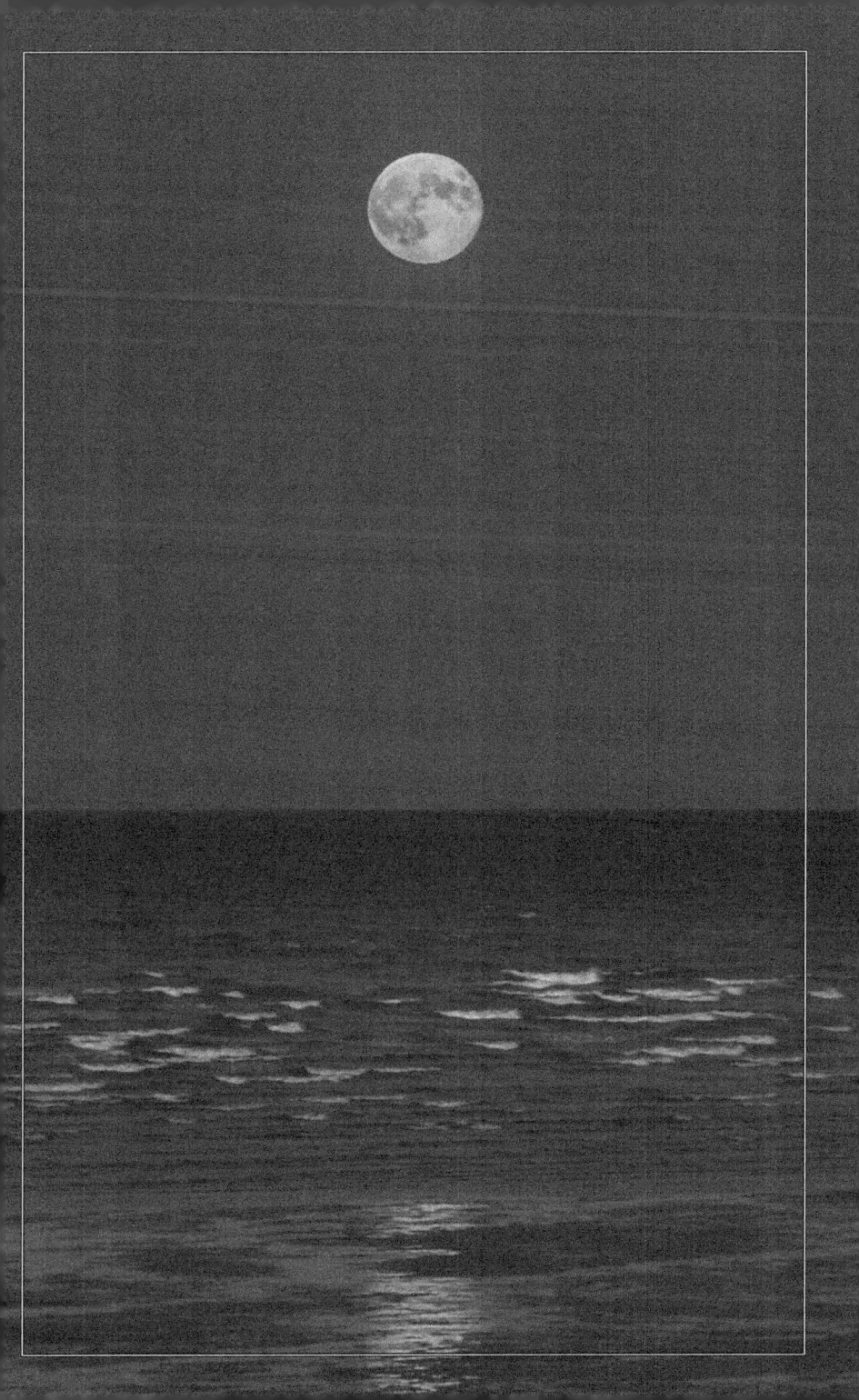

I am part of my whole

My spirit flags

When my body becomes weak

My heart is tied to my soul

And both are dependent

On each other to lift my spirit

This heartache cripples me

Lord, please heal me

Make me whole once again

———————

Whole

I never knew you
    You were that good
Your words flowed so easily
    So perfectly
Your smile even reached your eyes
    I wonder at the practice
    You have had to perfect this
Your hands so gentle
    So demanding
Your kiss so hungry
    So inviting
You were so broken
    That you broke me
How am I to forget
    And love again

———————

You

Gypsy Mercer

I gave you my heart years ago
Kept it warm with memories
And fantasy
I compared every man to you
The 'you' I envisioned in my dreams
Your smile
Your throaty whisper
Your blue eyes
Your smoldering passion
I kept you alive
Waiting for us to cross paths
Once again

Our love blossomed anew

As we reopened the door

With shared plans

And promises

Only too have them die on the vine

Short-lived

When our past did not match

The present

And you handed me back my heart

————————

Years Ago

Gypsy Mercer

Why do I mourn

The loss of a love

Not meant to be

Once perfect

Now tainted by life's decree

Only one chance

Be given you and me

Love hidden away in dreams

And fantasy

Seeking light

Seeking flight

Fresh hope

But we could not cope

With the devastation

Life had rained upon us

Rendering us

Too broken

To love again

_____

You and Me

I refuse to mourn
The loss of a love
Not meant for me
Rather I celebrate
Not dissolving into
Grief so debilitating
As to render me broken
   Instead merely bruised
Rather I gather
My sanity and stoicism
Having learned
A life lesson
To listen to my instincts
Over my heart

Merely Bruised

For two years

You kept me in limbo

At first

I assumed it was my insecurity

Your reassurances

Were lukewarm

But I wanted to believe

You were good

At dissimulation

You believed your lies

I was worth the effort

Your web

Spun and spun

I was trapped

Within my love

But then I woke

And saw you

Without your mask

And ran

Away

————————

Your Web

I put my trust in you

But trust in a five-letter word

One up from four

I should have known

You could not count

I believed in you

I believed in us

I believed your promises

Until they were proven lies

Then I died

    A bit

    A lot

Whilst picking up pieces

Of my unrecognizable heart

Turned blue from your freeze

Freeze

I wish I had not read you

Quite so well

The pain when you left my heart

Stopped me cold

I tried to pretend

That I did not see it

    The change on your face

    The stiffening of your posture

Your kiss was perfunctory

Your hug lacked tenderness

You added fuel to the debris

    In my soul

That fed my insecurities

Leaving a vacuum

Where once was love

Vacuum

Gypsy Mercer

Interior Art by:

Alev Takil
Austin Neill
Blake Wheeler
Crystal de Passille-Chabot
David Clode
Dream Capture
Ethan Dow
Igor Kasalovic
Jonathan Bean
Karl Frederickson
Kristopher Roller
Lance Asper
Laura Barry
Laura Summer
Nathan Dumlao
Nils Nedel
Pedro Lastra
Philippa Lowe
Rayuu Maldives
Summer Mahaffey
Todd Trapani
Zoltan Tasi

Via Unsplash

Who is Gypsy Mercer?

She is a girl that turned into a woman who read poetry and believed in Knights and magic.

Gypsy began writing in college when she found that her thoughts and written prose were so much more powerful than speaking the words.

Life and reality forced a hiatus while she raised a family and made her way into the professional world. All along, she believed that her real world was in opposition to the needs of her heart and her soul. No longer constrained, she picked up her pen freeing both.

This is the result of her escape from captivity into creativity.

Follow Gypsy Mercer
www.GypsyMercer.com
Facebook: GypsySong

Gypsy Mercer